Suzie's Seizure Guide

How to Help Friends in Need

Suzie's Seizure Guide

How to Help Friends in Need

Kara Rogers

gatekeeper press™
Columbus, OH

Suzie's Seizure Guide: How to Help Friends in Need

Published by Gatekeeper Press
2167 Stringtown Rd, Suite 109
Columbus, OH 43123-2989
www.GatekeeperPress.com

Illustrated by Timna Green

Library of Congress Control Number: 2021950099

ISBN (paperback): 9781662922428
ISBN (hardcover): 9781662922411
eISBN: 9781662922435

To Haddon Todd, my Epilepsy warrior

Hello, my name is Suzie. I'm at school today. It's almost my favorite part of the day—recess!

This is my best buddy Haddon. It's pronounced Had-don. We always play together during recess. I help look out for him. You see, Haddon has Epilepsy. Do you know what that is?

When someone has Epilepsy, they often have seizures. A seizure is when their brain doesn't work how it's supposed to. Your brain controls your whole body.

It helps you talk, walk, sing songs, and hop like a
kangaroo! For people with Epilepsy, their brain
can stop working properly out of nowhere!
That's when they have a seizure.

There are several different kinds of seizures. Sometimes Haddon falls down and shakes a lot, sometimes he can't breathe and turns blue, or sometimes he just stares off into space.

All of these things can be signs of a seizure.
Seizures can be very short or can last a
super long time!

Seizures can happen anytime and anywhere. But during the school day, we pay close attention to Haddon on the playground. He has to be careful, because if he gets too excited or too hot, he could have a seizure.

I look out for him on the playground. If I see him having a seizure, I run as fast as I can to tell the teacher.

"Haddon, are you okay? Oh no, he's having a seizure. Mrs. Murphy, come help!"

"I'm coming, Suzie!"

"Suzie, let's roll him on his side so he doesn't choke. May I have your jacket to put under his head? It will give him something soft to lay on. I'm also going to give him oxygen because he can't breathe very well. Let's check the time. If his seizure doesn't stop, we will need to give him special medicine."

"It looks like Haddon's seizure is over. Thanks for helping him, Suzie. We always have to be ready to help our friends, right?"

"That's right, Mrs. Murphy!"

Whew! I'm always a little nervous when Haddon has a seizure. But I'm so glad I could help my friend.

Remember how I said that during a seizure your brain doesn't work properly? Well, during seizures Haddon can't talk. He's not able to make his body do what he wants, and sometimes he urinates on himself. There's no need to laugh or point, though. Haddon can't control his body during a seizure.

Sometimes if seizures don't stop, he needs special medicine. When the seizure is over, the teacher can take good care of him and take him somewhere to rest.

After the seizure is over, Haddon can be very tired. It's best to just let him rest.

Once he's gotten the rest he needs, he's ready to play again.

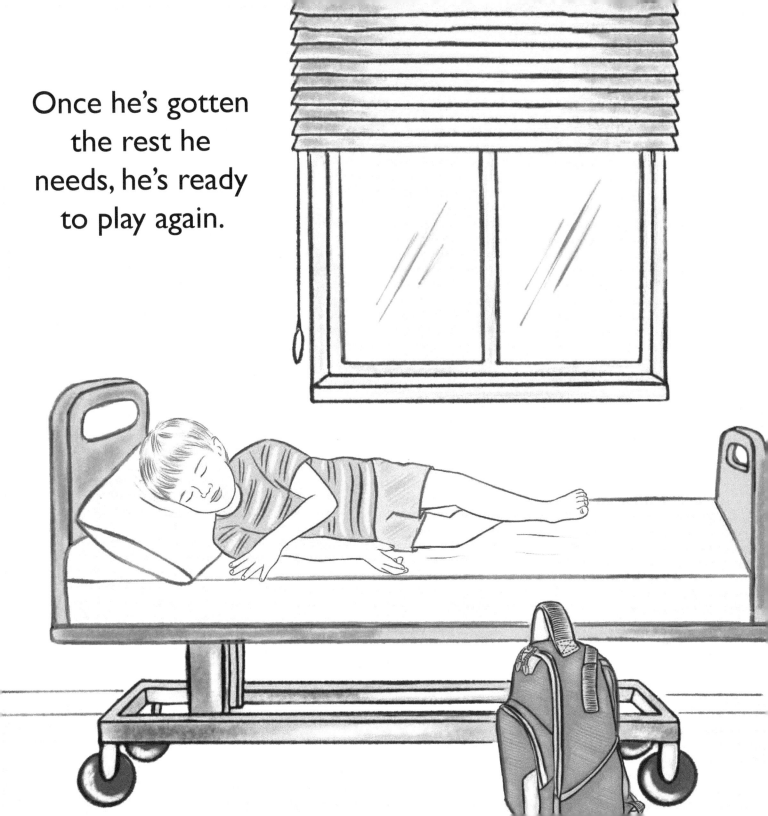

Have you ever been sick and had to take medicine to get better and stay well? Our friends who have seizures often take medicine and some even eat special foods to help keep seizures away and stay well. And every so often, they have to go to the hospital, and the doctor uses a big fancy machine to look at their brains. How cool is that?

Seizures can happen anytime, anywhere, so I always try to be as helpful as I can. There are a lot of people all over the world who have seizures and Epilepsy:

babies, little kids, big kids, adults, and even some famous people, like Theodore Roosevelt, the 26th President of the United States. It's good to know how to help them in case a seizure does happen.

It's also important to know that you can't catch seizures or Epilepsy like you can a cold or the flu. There are a lot of different reasons people have Epilepsy, but they didn't catch it from a friend. So, there's no need to be afraid of it!

There's a lot to learn about Epilepsy, more than I may ever understand. But here's Suzie's quick guide for what to do when you see someone having a seizure.

1. Find and tell a grown-up as fast as possible.

2. Roll the person having the seizure on their side. This helps them not choke.

3. Stay with them and call 911 if the seizure does not stop.

I may be little, but there's still something I can do to help. Thanks for learning about Epilepsy with me. I hope next time you see a friend having a seizure you remember this book and use these tips to be super helpful just like me.

Our Story:

When Haddon was four months old, we experienced his first seizure. It wasn't a "textbook" seizure, and we honestly had no idea that's what was happening. Two weeks later, he had a Tonic Clonic and thus began our journey with Epilepsy. Haddon has a rare form of Epilepsy called Dravet Syndrome. His seizures are incredibly difficult to treat and very resistant to medication. At the time of this publication, we are five years into this journey and it hasn't gotten any easier. However, as time has marched on, Haddon is learning and understanding with us. When we started looking into school options, we were given the opportunity to explain Haddon's condition to his classmates. But when I couldn't find any age appropriate books, that's when this book was born. I just knew this book needed to be written to explain Haddon's condition to himself, as well as to his new classmates who have never seen or even heard of Epilepsy or a seizure. My hope and prayer is that children will read this book and be understanding and compassionate toward others with seizures. I hope it gives them courage to help and knowledge of how to do so. The simple terms and explanations used in this book were written specifically for your little ones, so they can love my little one, and others like him, better.

Resource Page

Book Reference:

Ketogenic Diet Therapies for Epilepsy and Other Conditions by Dr. Eric Kossoff, Zahava Turner, Mackenzie C Cervenka, and Bobbie Barron

Online Resources:

www.epilepsy.com

https://charliefoundation.org

www.ketodietcalculator.org

www.matthewsfriends.org

Lightning Source UK Ltd.
Milton Keynes UK
UKHW020231240322
400505UK00005B/207